Don't miss the other books in this series:
THE RAINBOW FISH
RAINBOW FISH TO THE RESCUE!
RAINBOW FISH AND THE BIG BLUE WHALE

Copyright © 2001 by Nord-Süd Verlag AG, Gossau Zürich, Switzerland
First published in Switzerland under the title *Der Regenbogenfisch hat keine Angst mehr*.
English translation copyright © 2001 by North-South Books Inc.

First published in the United States, Great Britain, Canada,
Australia, and New Zealand in 2001 by North-South Books,
an imprint of Nord-Süd Verlag AG, Gossau Zürich, Switzerland.

Distributed in the United States by North-South Books Inc., New York.

Library of Congress Cataloging-in-Publication Data is available.
ISBN 0-439-32713-X
1 3 5 7 9 TB 10 8 6 4 2
Printed in Belgium

For more information about our books, and the authors and artists
who create them, visit our web site: www.northsouth.com

MARCUS PFISTER

RAINBOW FISH
AND THE
SEA MONSTERS' CAVE

TRANSLATED BY J. ALISON JAMES

NORTH-SOUTH BOOKS
NEW YORK / LONDON

"Help! Come quick!" The little blue fish was alarmed. His friends were there in a minute. "What is it? What's wrong?"

"Look at the bumpy-backed fish. He must be sick. He isn't moving, and he doesn't answer me. He just groans."

"Let me through," said the swordfish. She went up to the bumpy-backed fish. "Can you tell me what's wrong?"

The bumpy-backed fish moaned. "My stomach aches. I feel terrible."

"You need red algae," said the swordfish.

"But the only place where red algae grows is on the other side of the sea monsters' cave," said the little blue fish.

"I'll go," declared Rainbow Fish.

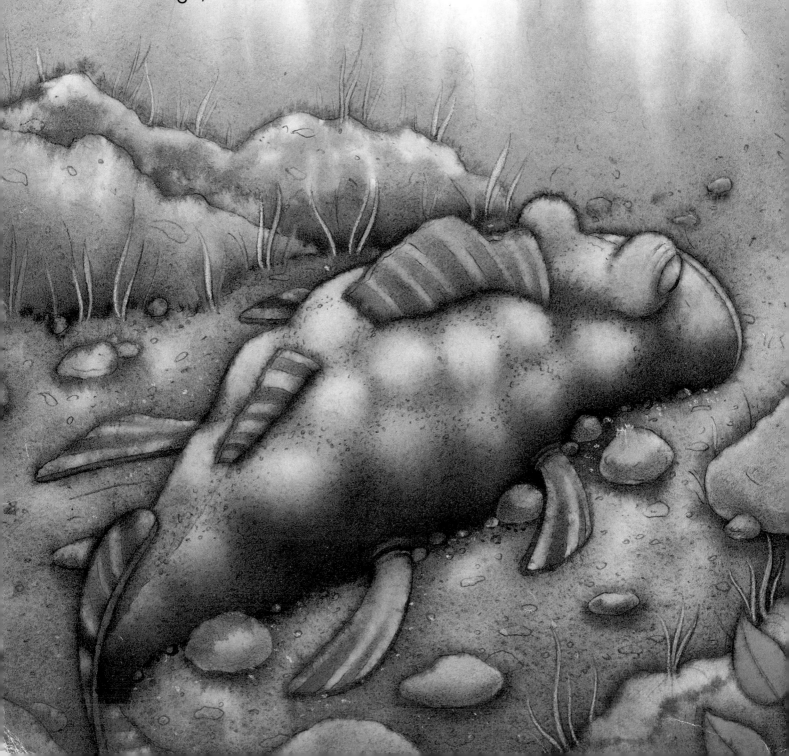

"Are you out of your mind?" cried the others.
"It's the most dangerous place in the entire ocean!"
"That's where the rock monsters live!"
"And a creature with a thousand arms to catch you!"
"And the five-eyed globe fish!"

Rainbow Fish trembled. He almost changed his mind.
But then he looked at the poor bumpy-backed fish
lying in the sand. Bravely he said, "I'll go anyway."
"I'll come with you," cried the little blue fish.
That made Rainbow Fish feel better. Quickly they
swam off before they lost their nerve.

The sea monsters' cave was dark and frightening. The rock walls were steep and jagged.

"Swim lower!" whispered Rainbow Fish. "That rock monster has his mouth open to eat us!"

The cave grew even darker.

Suddenly the little blue fish cried out, "Help!
The thousand-arm creature has caught me!"
Rainbow Fish tugged and pulled until his friend
slipped out of the monster's slimy arms. That was
a close call. Now he was really scared.

Rainbow Fish looked down. "The five-eyed globe fish is watching us," he whispered.

The little blue fish shivered. "Quick, let's get out of here!" he said, and they swam as fast as they could until they finally emerged on the other side of the sea monsters' cave.

There they saw a big clump of red algae! The two friends picked as much as they could carry, and then they turned to go.

The little blue fish hesitated. "I can't go back through the cave. I'm too scared."

Rainbow Fish was scared too, but he said, "At least now we know what's in there."

They looked at each other, gathered their courage, and swam off. Soon they saw the five-eyed globe fish.

"There's something funny about those eyes," said Rainbow Fish, and he swam a little closer.

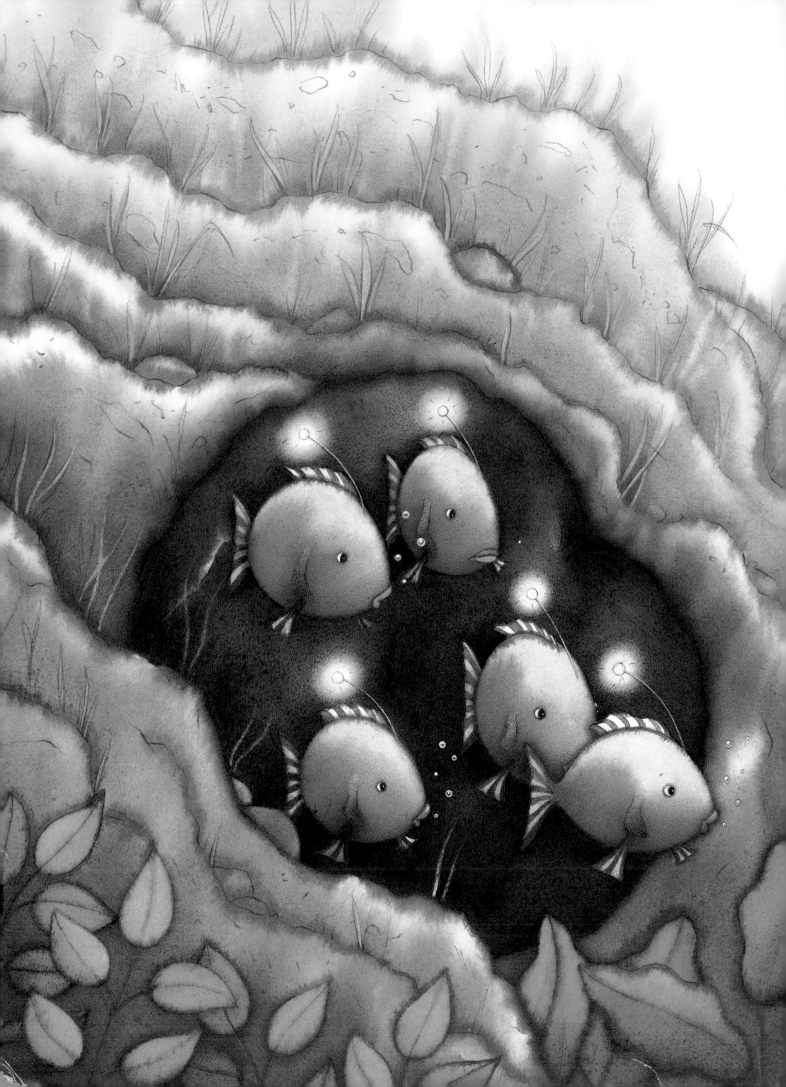

Then Rainbow Fish laughed. "That isn't a five-eyed globe fish," he said. "It's just the lanterns from five little lantern fish!"

"Why, they aren't scary at all!" said the little blue fish, giggling with relief.

When they reached the creature with a thousand arms, they looked more closely.

"Seaweed!" they said together and laughed.

The rock monsters turned out to be just ordinary rocks. Unafraid, the two fish swam right by them and out of the cave to find their friends.

"You made it!" the other fish cried.

"Did you see the rock monsters?"

"Did anything try to eat you?"

"We'll tell you everything later," answered Rainbow Fish. "But first we have to give this red algae to the bumpy-backed fish."

The bumpy-backed fish nibbled at the algae and soon he felt better. "I don't know how I can thank you. It must have been dreadful to go through the cave."

"We were terribly afraid," Rainbow Fish admitted. "But when we looked more closely—"

"The monsters disappeared!" interrupted the little blue fish happily.

And then the two of them told the story of their journey and all the terrifying monsters that weren't really monsters at all.